Why Does It Have To Rain?

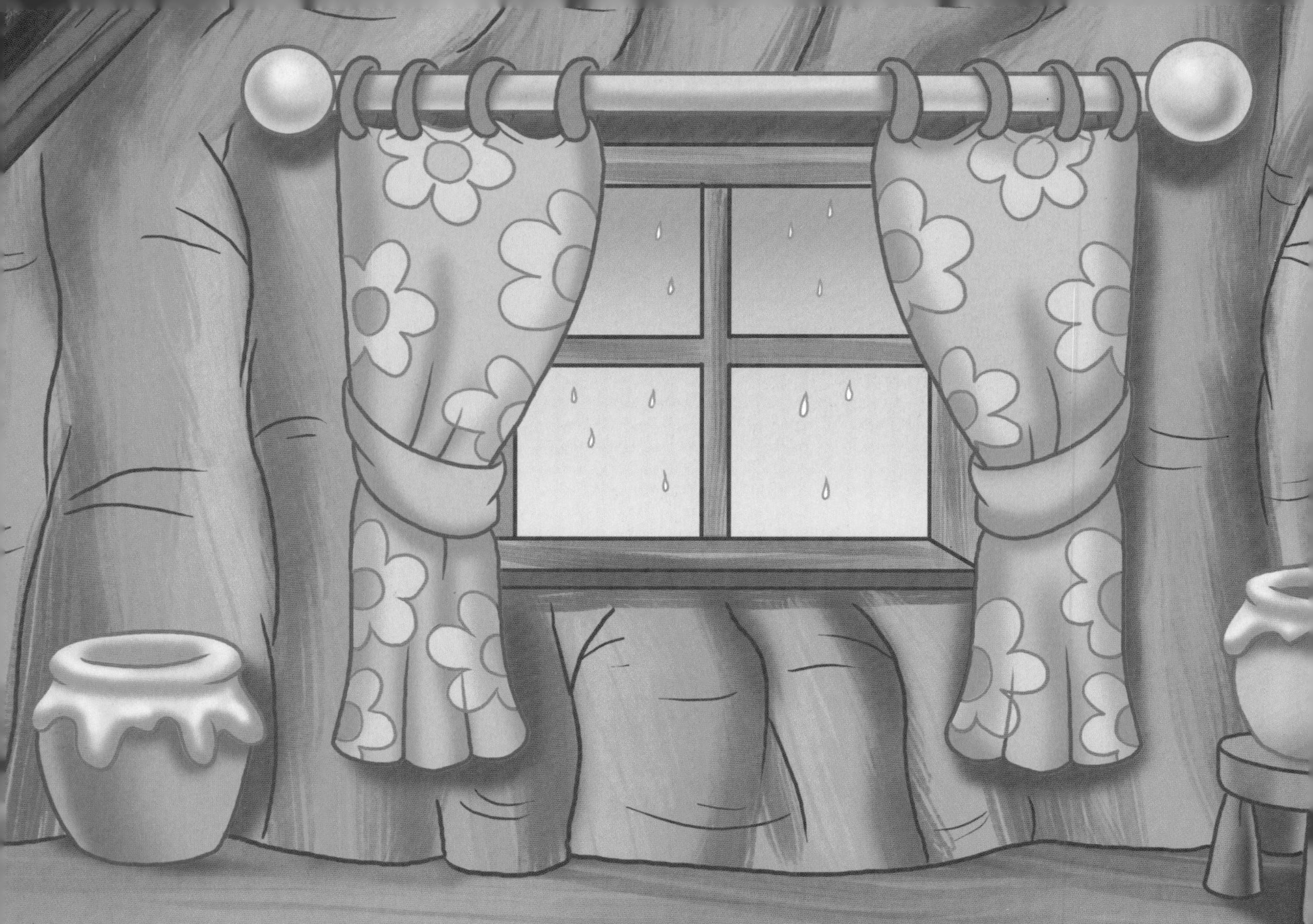

Pooh had a big smile on his face. He was dreaming about going on a picnic with his friends—which is exactly what he was supposed to do when he woke up.

RAT-A-TAT-TAT! A noise startled Pooh from his slumber.

"Morning already?" he thought as he climbed out of bed. He glanced out the window. "But where is the sun?"

When Pooh opened the door, there was nothing to greet him but a sky full of big, gray clouds and a light drizzle of rain. RAT-A-TAT-TAT! Pooh heard it again. It was the sound of raindrops falling on his roof.

"Rain! Oh, bother!" said Pooh. "I hope we can still go on our picnic."

“Perhaps Piglet will know whether we are going on the picnic or not,” thought Pooh. And so, after having a little smackerel of honey for breakfast and getting dressed, he headed off to see his friend.

As Pooh got closer to Piglet’s house, he heard singing.

“Piglet!” cried Pooh when he discovered his friend. “What are you doing?”
“I’m taking a rain shower,” answered Piglet. “I love the rain, don’t you?”
“Not really,” Pooh replied. “Not if it means we can’t go on our picnic. Why does it have to rain? I don’t like getting wet.”

"It rains to make everything nice and clean—including very small animals!" Piglet explained cheerily.

Pooh thought about this for a moment. And, being a bear of very little brain, he had to think some more. Finally, he decided that Piglet was right. The Hundred-Acre Wood always did look pretty and clean after a rainstorm.

The two friends couldn't decide whether they should go on their picnic or not. It wasn't raining hard, but it wasn't stopping either. They headed off to see what Roo might want to do.

Little Roo was outside catching raindrops on his tongue. "Come on! Try it!" invited Roo.

Pooh and Piglet opened their mouths and stuck out their tongues.

"Well, the rain doesn't taste as good as honey," Pooh announced. "But it is nice and tickly."

Kanga opened the window.

"Roo!" she called. "Come inside and put on your raincoat and boots, please."

At just that moment, Tigger came bouncing by. He landed with a SPLASH right outside the open window.

"I love rain!" announced Tigger as he jumped into another puddle. "It makes everything all splishy-splashy!"

"Yes, Tigger dear, it certainly does," said Kanga. "Especially me."

"Let's play 'Follow the Tigger!'" suggested Roo.

So the friends lined up and jumped from puddle to puddle right behind their bouncy pal.

Next they made mud pies.

"Mine will be the bestest," declared Tigger, "because I use only the muddiest mud!"

“I am definitely going to need another shower,” Piglet said.

“Hmmm,” thought Pooh. “Maybe it doesn’t rain to make things clean. Maybe it rains to make puddles and mud for us to get dirty in instead.”

After a while, Pooh's tummy rumbled.

"I was just wondering," he said anxiously, "if we are still going on our picnic today."

"Not if I have to eat soggy sandwiches," declared Tigger. "Yuck!"

"But maybe it will stop raining," Piglet added.

"Let's go ask Rabbit," suggested Roo. "He seems to know an awful lot about the weather."

“I certainly hope it won’t stop drizzling,” Rabbit told the friends as they stood by his garden. “I love rain! It makes everything grow!”

“Grow! Oh, goody!” cried Piglet. The very small animal measured himself against his friend.

“Pooh,” he asked, “do I look any taller?”

“No, Piglet,” Rabbit said. “The rain won’t make *you* grow, but it will make plants grow.”

“Oh,” thought Pooh. “Maybe it doesn’t rain to make things clean or to make puddles and mud to play in. Maybe it has to rain so Rabbit’s garden will grow.”

Rabbit taught the friends a little something about plants, but he couldn't tell them whether the rain would stay or go.

"Let's ask Christopher Robin what he thinks about a picnic today," Rabbit suggested. "He always knows what to do."

The friends found Christopher Robin sailing his boat in the stream. "Ahoy, there!" Christopher Robin called. "Where are you off to?"

“Well,” Pooh began, “we’re trying to decide whether to go on a picnic today. What do you think?”

“I think sunny days are better picnic days than rainy ones,” said Christopher Robin. “How about a game of Pooh Sticks instead?”

The friends walked up onto the bridge and threw their Pooh Sticks into the stream.

"Christopher Robin," said Pooh as he watched the sticks float by, "why do you think it has to rain?"

"Well, I think it has to rain so that the stream stays full of water. And we need the stream for frogs and fish to live in and for boats to sail on," Christopher Robin explained.

"And for Pooh Sticks to float in," added Roo.

Christopher Robin had given Pooh a lot to think about—so much that Pooh excused himself and went off to his Thinking Spot.

"Think, think, think!" Pooh told himself. "Why does it have to rain?"

Was it to make everything nice and clean? Was it so there would be puddles to splash and play in? Was it to make Rabbit's garden grow? Was it to fill up the stream?

Finally, Pooh was all thought out.

"I know!" he said suddenly. "Rain is good for lots of things!"

He looked up and saw a rainbow stretching across the sky. Seconds later, a ray of sunshine beamed through the clouds and shone right on Pooh's Thinking Spot.

"I know one more reason for the rain," Pooh announced to himself. "To make us glad for a beautiful, sunny day!"

Make It Rain!

Why does it have to rain? The process begins when the sun heats water in oceans, rivers, and other bodies of water. The water evaporates, turning into a vapor or mist that goes into the air. As the water vapor cools, it condenses and forms clouds. When the clouds become too full to hold any more condensation—which consists of water droplets—it rains or sleets or snows, depending on the temperature. The water then falls to Earth, and the process starts all over again.

This hands-on activity demonstrates this cycle in miniature—building young children's observation skills while at the same time teaching them about cause and effect.

You can make your own rain shower in a glass! Here's all you have to do:

Step 1: Fill a drinking glass or jar halfway with water.

Step 2: Cover the glass or jar tightly with plastic wrap and secure it with a rubber band.

Step 3: Place your glass in the refrigerator until little beads of water form on the plastic wrap.

Step 4: Take the glass out of the refrigerator and put it on a counter or table. As the glass and the water inside warm up, the beads of water will "rain" down from the glass back into the water.